THIS WALKER BOOK BELONGS TO:

_____

_____

_____

_____

For Winifred Clarke
with thanks

M.M.

First published 1992 by Walker Books Ltd
87 Vauxhall Walk, London SE11 5HJ

This edition published 2002

2 4 6 8 10 9 7 5 3 1

Text © 1992 Michelle Magorian
Illustrations © 1992 Jan Ormerod

This book has been typeset in Garamond

Printed in Hong Kong

British Library Cataloguing in Publication Data:
a catalogue record for this book is available
from the British Library

ISBN 0-7445-8961-4

JUMP!

MICHELLE MAGORIAN

illustrated by

JAN ORMEROD

WALKER BOOKS

AND SUBSIDIARIES

LONDON • BOSTON • SYDNEY

Every Saturday morning,
Steven sat with his father and
watched his older sister,
Theresa, at her ballet class.
There were three boys in the
class – Michael, Joe and Barry.
Steven longed to join them.
When the boys and girls jumped,
Steven leaned forward and
pretended he was jumping too.
After the class he danced with
Theresa all the way home.

One day, when the boys and girls were bending their knees at the barre, Steven overheard the teacher saying, "Remember, class, the deeper you can plié, the higher you will be able to jump." Steven watched even more closely. Jumping was the thing he liked doing best.

As soon as
he was
home he
practised.

In
the hall.

In the
kitchen.

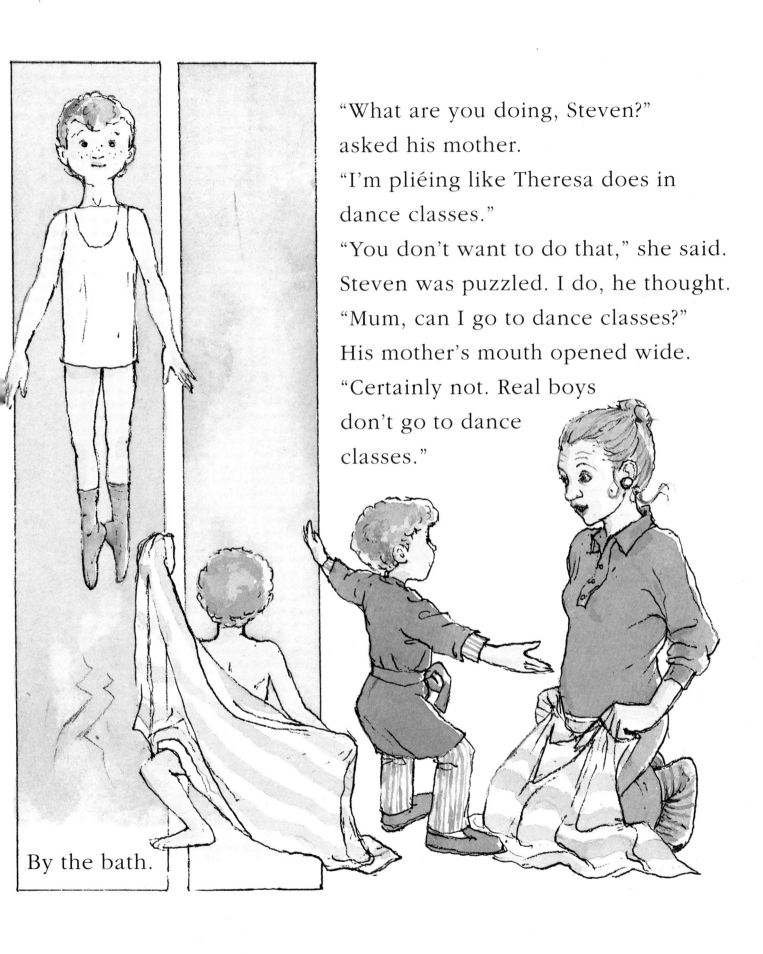

"What are you doing, Steven?"
asked his mother.
"I'm pliéing like Theresa does in
dance classes."
"You don't want to do that," she said.
Steven was puzzled. I do, he thought.
"Mum, can I go to dance classes?"
His mother's mouth opened wide.
"Certainly not. Real boys
don't go to dance
classes."

By the bath.

The following Saturday, after the
class had done their bows and curtsies,
Steven walked over to where the boys
were putting on their tracksuits.

He squeezed Michael's arm, he touched
Joe's back and he gave Barry's hair a tug.
"What are you doing?" they asked.
"I'm seeing if you're real," said Steven.
"Well, we are," they said.

"They are real, Mum," he told his mother.
"You can play basketball," she said, looking
up from the television, "and that's that."
"What's basketball?"
"A game, a tough game, with a ball," she
said, and pointed at the screen. "Look."

"They're jumping!" he exclaimed.

"Yes," said his mum, "as high as they can."

"Good," said Steven. "Can I play it today?"

"We don't have a ball or a net, and you need somewhere to play it," she said.

"You'll have to grow a bit too."

"Oh," Steven sighed,
disappointed. He raced
into his and Theresa's
bedroom and pliéd and
leapt and flung his arms
as wildly as he could until
he felt better.

At the next class, when
the boys were jumping, Steven
couldn't sit still any longer.
He ran across the floor.
His father tried to pull him away.
"Let him stay," said the teacher.
"He's good."
After the jumps the teacher said,
"Show me what else you
can do, Steven."
So he did.

The children clapped.
"Would you like to be in
the show this year?" the
teacher asked.
"Will you teach me a basketball
dance?" asked Steven.
The teacher laughed.
"Well," she said, "I'll see."

On the night of the show,
Steven's mum and dad sat in the audience.
"Where's Steven?" his mum asked.
"He's here," said Steven's father.
"Where? I can't see him."

"You will. Later. It's a surprise."
The lights went down and the curtains opened.
There was a bumble-bee dance by the babies,
followed by a skating dance.
"It's Theresa's class next," whispered Dad.

They heard a referee's whistle and
music, then all the boys and girls
danced on stage in shorts and T-shirts.
The children spun and threw an
imaginary basketball at one another.
They jumped in all directions, patting
it around each other in circles.

Theresa, playing the referee,
whirled in and out through
the teams with her whistle,
until one team had won and
the dance was over.

The smallest and
happiest person
in the group leapt
the highest.
It was Steven.

The audience laughed and cheered.
Steven's mum was the only person not clapping.
She was too surprised even to speak.
"That small one with the red hair and freckles,
why, he can almost fly," said a woman in front of them.
"That's our Steven," said his father loudly.
The woman turned round.
"He can certainly jump, can't he?" she said, astonished.
Steven's mum was still watching the children bowing
on stage. Steven waved. His mother waved back.

"He'll make a fine basketball player one day," said the woman. "A fine player." "Yes, I think he will," said Steven's mum, and she smiled proudly. "He'll make a fine dancer too."

MICHELLE MAGORIAN says her inspiration for *Jump!* came from
the comments people used to make about her eldest son when he was still
in nappies. "I was surprised to hear people talking about all the 'boyish'
activities he would take part in when he was older and thought, 'What if
my son preferred dance to rugby?'," she says. "In this mood, I wrote a story
about a little boy who felt most alive and happy when he was dancing,
and about his frustrations when he was 'advised' against doing it
by someone he loved."

Michelle Magorian is best known for her novel *Goodnight Mister Tom*, which
won three literary awards and became a BAFTA-winning television film
starring John Thaw. She has written several other novels for young people,
including *Back Home* (also televised); *Cuckoo in the Nest*; *A Little Love Song*;
and *A Spoonful of Jam*. Michelle lives in Hampshire with her family.

JAN ORMEROD says of *Jump!*, "I love to watch children dance, and I love
to draw children dancing, so it was great fun illustrating this book."

Jan Ormerod won several major awards for her first book, *Sunshine*.
She has since written and illustrated many books for children, including the
Walker titles *Happy Christmas Gemma*, which was shortlisted for the Smarties
Prize; *Eat Up, Gemma*, its follow-up; and *One Ballerina Two*. Jan was born
and brought up in Western Australia but now lives in Cambridge, England.